To My Ava,
Love,
Grandma

July 09

If I Could

Susan Milord

illustrated by

Christopher Denise

CANDLEWICK PRESS
CAMBRIDGE, MASSACHUSETTS

If I could,
I'd rouse the sun

and make it shine
till day is done.

If I could,
I'd paint the flowers

to brighten all
your waking hours.

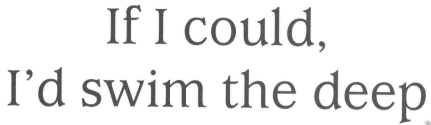

If I could,
I'd swim the deep

in search of treasures
for you to keep.

If I could,
I'd sing a song

to make the stars wink
all night long.

If I could,
I'd make you see

how very much
you mean to me.

You are the song.

You are the light—

a treat
and
a treasure,

a joy and delight.

This much I know,
this much is true

I couldn't love you
more than I do.

But if I could,
I would.

For my mother,
with a bushel and a peck
and a hug around the neck — S. M.

For Anika, Sofia, and Isabel — C. D.

Text copyright © 2008 by Susan Milord
Illustrations copyright © 2008 by Christopher Denise

First edition 2008

This edition published specially for Books Are Fun 2008 by Candlewick Press, Inc.

Library of Congress Cataloging-in-Publication Data is available.

Library of Congress Catalog Card Number pending

ISBN 978-0-7636-2348-7 (Candlewick trade edition)
ISBN 978-0-7636-4069-9 (Books Are Fun edition)

Printed in China

This book was typeset in Usherwood.
The illustrations were done in acrylic and charcoal.

Candlewick Press
2067 Massachusetts Avenue
Cambridge, Massachusetts 02140

visit us at www.candlewick.com